Michael

Michael

The world is waiting for YOU

Love + Light

David

I hope you and your children
have fun exploring the continents
and seeking for the lost bug!!

Erica

There's a World in my House by David Wood

Copyright © 2005 by David Wood. All rights reserved.

Published in the United States of America
by Tate Publishing, LLC
127 East Trade Center Terrace
Mustang, OK 73064
(888) 361–9473

ISBN: 1–9332909–0-0
Printed in Korea

There's a World in my House

by David Wood
Illustrated by Erica Dissler

Tate Publishing, LLC

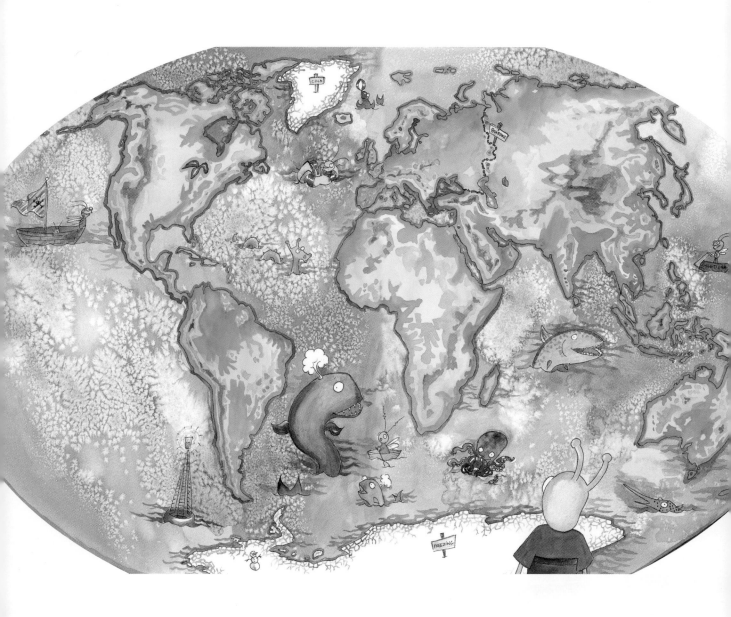

Dedication:

This book is dedicated to my two wonderful sons,
Calvin and Benjamin.
You are my teachers, my best friends,
my inspiration and my wrestling buddies.
Thank you for being who you are, and let's never forget
to always "look for the mystery."

 I love you,
Daddy.

Acknowledgments:

Special thanks to Pamela for your love, truth, strength, creativity and light. Thanks also go to "Teacher" Maxine Hawes for your gentle guidance and truly amazing gift with children, and to all of my friends that make my life so rich and fun.

Of all the continents around the world,
I haven't seen a lot.
But then, I'm only 5 years old,
And Dad said "Traveling, you are not!"

"Why can't I travel?" I asked him,
he just gave me a funny look.
He said, "If you really want to see the world,
You can study it in a book."

"In a book," I scowled and I stomped away,
"but I don't know how to read."
"You don't have to," my Mom said,
"it's a tour guide, that you'll need."

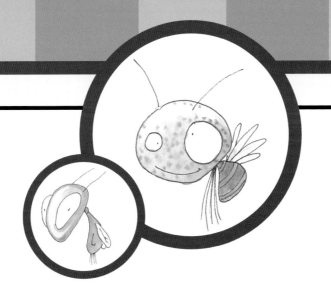

"What's that?" she heard me mumble,
and with that she disappeared.
There was a bang, and a crash, and a little squeal,
And Mom came back, wearing a long false beard.

"I am John your tour guide," she said in a big deep voice.
"The world is waiting for you, which continent is your choice?"
Now the beard didn't really fool me, I knew it was still my mom.
But I pretended anyhow, and boy did we have fun.

In Africa we went on Safari,
John turned up all the heat.
We made binoculars from toilet rolls
Look John! There's an elephant, with shoes on his feet.

Then we went to Antarctica,
with the freezer door open, I nearly froze.
With the ice cubes we made a penguin,
and I kept getting a runny nose.

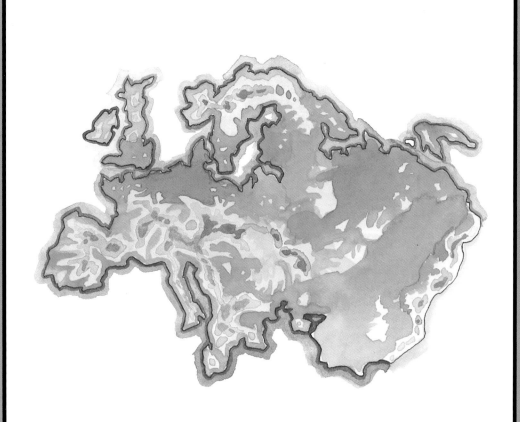

Next we made two long ears
and a little white tail to wear.
I hopped and ran as fast as I could,
just like a European hare.

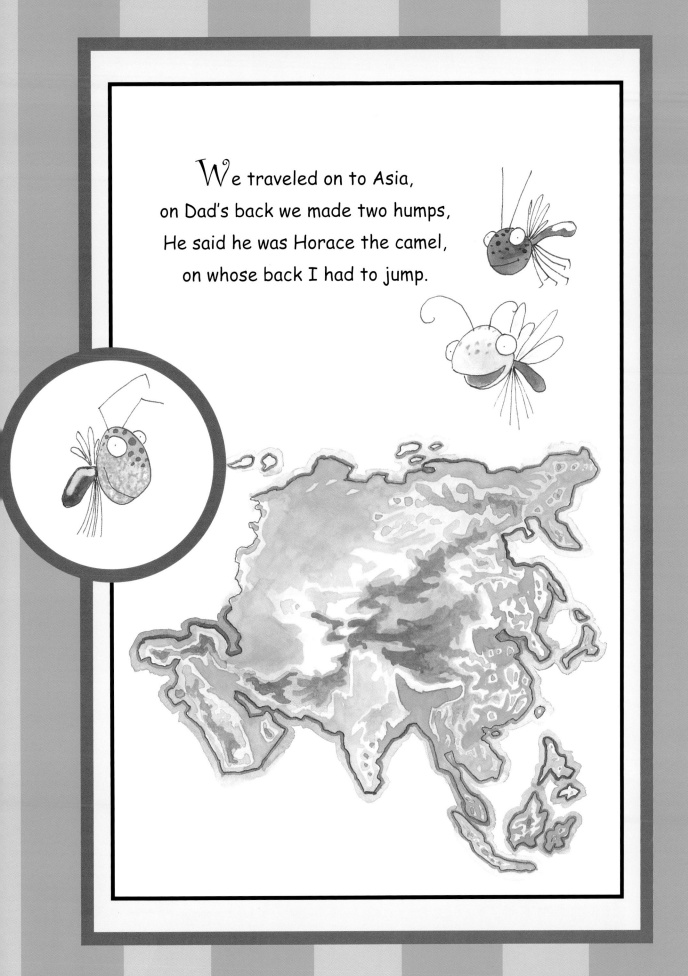

We traveled on to Asia,
on Dad's back we made two humps,
He said he was Horace the camel,
on whose back I had to jump.

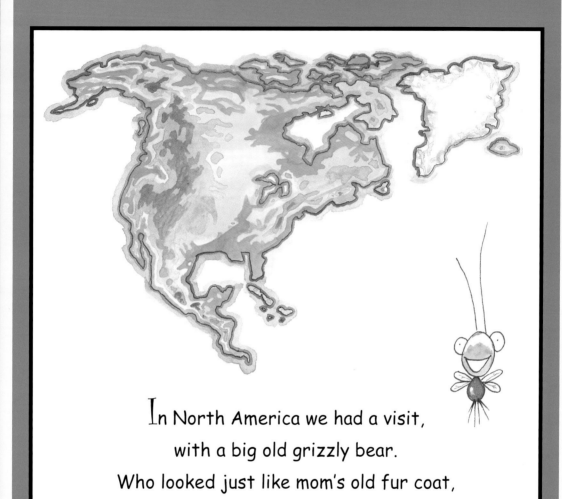

In North America we had a visit,
with a big old grizzly bear.
Who looked just like mom's old fur coat,
the one she used to wear.

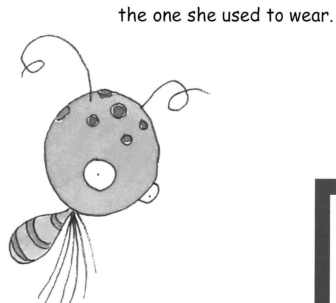

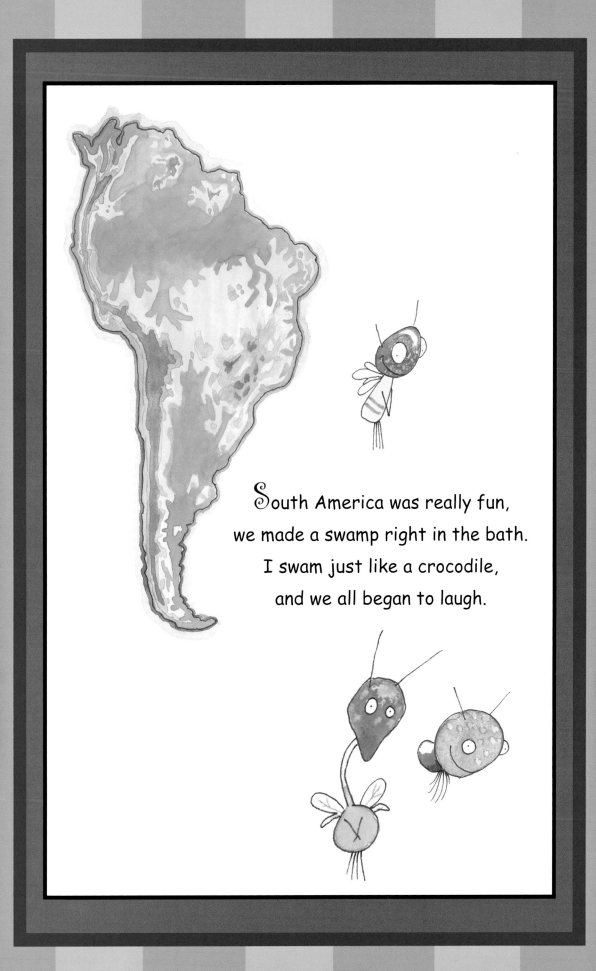

South America was really fun,
we made a swamp right in the bath.
I swam just like a crocodile,
and we all began to laugh.

John told me about Australia,
and he described a kangaroo.
On my coat we sewed a pocket,
so I could be one too.

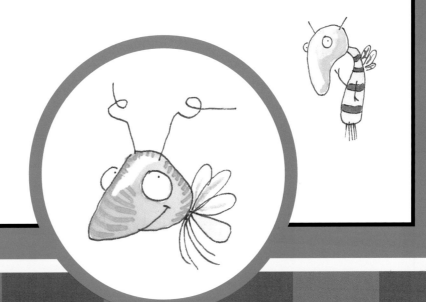

We had visited the seven continents,
and we repeated their names out loud.
I practised until I was sleepy,
and I felt extremely proud.

North America,
South America,
Africa, Europe, Asia,
Australia and Antarctica.

It was time for me to go to bed;
we'd had a really special day!
Now I really want to see the world,
and know I can, each time I play.

John promised that he would come back soon,
"because there's so much more to see."
He said it was time to close my eyes,
because my dreams, were waiting for me.

As I closed my eyes I thought to myself,
our world is nicely weird.
Mom's kiss goodnight really tickled me;
she forgot to take off her beard.

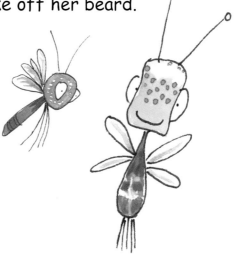

Can you find Eric?

Please go back now and study each picture in this book
and see if you can find where Eric is hiding.
You will have to look really carefully because he is a shy
little bug and only his head is showing.
Each time you find him, don't forget to shout really loud,
"I Found Eric!" Good Luck.

Time for a quiz.

What is the tour guide's name?

How many continents are there?

Which animal in the story is found in Africa?

What did John (Mom) make out of toilet rolls?

What continent is home to the penguin?

Which animal had two long ears and a little white tail?

Which animal in the story is found in North America?

Which animal played in the bath?

Which continent is home to the kangaroo?

What did Mom forget to take off?

Name all seven continents.

Great Job!

Now match each animal below with the continent it lives in.

Elephant   Europe

Penguin   Asia

Hare   Australia

Camel   Antarctica

Crocodile   North America

Kangaroo   South America

Grizzly Bear   Africa

Make up a story about your two favourite animals.

You are amazing!!

How many bugs can you find in this book?

Wow, well done!
Come back and read me again soon.

35

The

End

Contact author David Wood

www.davidwoodtraining.com

To order more copies of this book, contact

TATE PUBLISHING, LLC

127 East Trade Center Terrace

Mustang, Oklahoma 73064

(888) 361 - 9473

Tate Publishing, LLC

www.tatepublishing.com